WELCOME
TO
BROG

BROG BYPASS

Oxford University Press, Walton Street, Oxford OX2 6DP

Oxford is a trade mark of Oxford University Press

Text copyright © Jean Hood 1994
Illustrations copyright © Peter Kavanagh 1994
First published 1994

A CIP catalogue record for this book is available from the British Library

ISBN 0 19 279965 7

Printed in Hong Kong

For Adrian, with love   J. H.

For Mum and Dad   P. K.

The Dragon of Brog

Jean Hood

Illustrated by Peter Kavanagh

Oxford University Press

King Criss and his daughter, Lisa, were very poor. Their clothes were worn, the furniture had woodworm, and the tapestries on the palace walls were threadbare. As for the palace itself, bits were always falling off. The roofs leaked, tiles blew off the turrets, and the drawbridge was too weak to raise, so it was always left down. Anyway, King Criss thought it made the palace more welcoming.

Not that there were any guests to welcome. Nobody important ever bothered to visit the Kingdom of Brog.

One day the Chancellor said to the King, 'You must collect taxes from the people.'

'Don't be silly,' answered the King, 'they have no money.'

'But, Sire, you must do something for Princess Lisa. No prince has ever asked to marry her.'

'But no prince has ever seen her!' retorted the King.

'And why is that?' cried the Chancellor, banging his hand on the table. 'Because the roads are rivers of mud and the palace is likely to fall down at any moment!'

Suddenly a page rushed in. 'There's a dragon!' he shouted. 'A real fire-breathing dragon!'

'Nonsense,' said the King. 'There are no dragons left.'

But when he went out on to the balcony he was just in time to see the dragon disappear behind a hill, and he found hundreds of his people gathered below, begging him to save them from the terrible creature.

Their voices made the whole palace shake alarmingly, so the King promised to do something about the dragon, if only they would be quiet.

'And what will you do, father?' asked Princess Lisa.
'Send for a dragon-slayer, of course,' answered the King.
'Not a hope,' said the Chancellor. 'The last one died years ago.'

'Never mind,' said Princess Lisa,
who was a very sensible girl,
too sensible to be a fairy-tale
princess. 'If we don't bother the
dragon it will probably leave us
in peace.'

The story of the dragon spread far and wide, not only in Brog but through all the neighbouring lands where many famous knights dreamed of slaying the terrible Last Dragon. They set out with their squires, their families, and their servants, and squelched through the mud. There were no inns, so they brought tents with them, and the farmers of Brog were only too pleased to hire out their fields as camp sites for the visitors.

The first to arrive at King Criss's palace was the renowned warrior Sir Prize. He was rather muddy from his journey, but the King made him welcome and was delighted to have company at last.

After dinner, Sir Prize stood up to make his grand speech: 'Sire, your kingdom has been ravaged by a loathsome dragon. I have come to rid you of the beast. What is the reward?'

'Reward?' gulped the King, as he remembered that he had no money. Then he had a brilliant idea. 'Oh, the REWARD! Of course! The hand of Princess Lisa in marriage.'

'Not likely!' said Princess Lisa to herself.
'This isn't a fairy story.'

Next morning, Sir Prize
mounted his white charger,
took up his lance,
and rode to meet the dragon.

But Sir Prize had never seen a real dragon before, and when
the creature rushed out of its lair, breathing smoke and fire
from its nostrils, and roaring blood-curdling roars,
all his courage left him, and he turned and fled
without even stopping at the palace to say goodbye.

'Oh dear,' said Princess Lisa with a grin.
'That was a nasty surprise for him, wasn't it?'

The next to present himself was a very proud, fat knight named
Sir Cumference. He was so round that when he put on his black armour
he looked just like a huge cannon-ball on legs.

'Fear not, Sire,' he said to the King as he was winched on to his steed.
'I will be back in no time at all.' . . .

WHAK!

. . . And so he was.

The poor knight

rolled all the way

down the hill

and fell into

the moat with

a SPLASH!

By now even more visitors had arrived in Brog to see the dragon for themselves — at a safe distance, of course. Field after field was covered in tents, new markets sprang up, and the craftsmen of Brog worked night and day to make dragon souvenirs. The people became extremely rich.

Then came the magnificent knight, Sir Render, in his shining armour.
'Show me this beast!' he thundered. 'Here in my hand I hold the
ancient sword Dragonbane, the Blade-That-Cannot-Be-Broken!'

And he spoke the truth: the fearsome sword could not be broken . . .

. . . Instead, it melted at the first blast of fiery breath, and he was forced to surrender. The dragon took all his armour and made him walk home in his underwear.

Last of all came Sir Vuright.

'I don't trust this one,' thought Princess Lisa, so she stayed awake, and caught him sneaking out of the castle with his squires at dead of night. One of the squires was pushing a large wooden keg.

Princess Lisa followed them all the way to the dragon's lair, where they set down the keg and lit a fuse.

'Gunpowder! That's not fair!' she muttered angrily, and as they ran away down the hill she kicked the burning barrel after them. Just as it overtook them it exploded: BANG!

'And serve you right!' exclaimed Princess Lisa.

Suddenly a deep voice boomed, 'I'm glad someone is on my side.'

The Princess looked round, and there stood the dragon, pale and shimmering in the moonlight. 'Of course I am,' she said. 'I don't want to marry any of those stupid knights, so I've got to stop them from slaying you.'

'I see,' said the dragon thoughtfully. 'Do you know why I came to Brog?'

'No,' answered Princess Lisa.

'I thought I'd be safe here because Brog was so poor that nobody ever bothered with it. Ah well. For both our sakes I'll go away.'

'No don't!' cried the Princess. 'I've got a great idea.'

Next morning, she came down to breakfast looking very pleased with herself. 'Father,' she began, 'I want to talk to you about the dragon.'

'Fear not, my child,' said King Criss. 'Soon a gallant knight will rid us of this terrible curse.'

'What terrible curse?' demanded the Princess. 'The dragon isn't a curse, it's a valuable economic resource.'

'A what?' interrupted the Chancellor.

'Something that's making Brog rich,' explained the Princess, who understood such things much better than the Chancellor and the King. 'Our people are earning oodles of money, and if you collect the taxes we could have proper roads, lovely clothes, and a truly royal palace with inside loos. While Brog is home to the Last Dragon, people will come from all over the world and pay to see it.'

So King Criss turned Brog into a National Park, and passed a law forbidding anyone to slay the dragon.

Other rare creatures — phoenixes, griffins, and unicorns — also came to live in Brog where they were safe from hunters.

Visitors arrived in their thousands: they stayed in the luxurious new inns, and went home laden with souvenirs. The dragon was so pleased that he regularly flew round Dragon Hill breathing fire to impress the tourists.

Princess Lisa had seen quite enough of gallant knights. She married a handsome accountant, and lived happily ever after.